The Truth About OLD PEOPLE

Elina Ellis

TW🕷 HOOTS

My grandparents are *really* old.

They have wrinkly faces,
a little bit of hair, and funny teeth.

I've been hearing lots of strange things about old people.

Some people say old people are

NOT MUCH FUN.

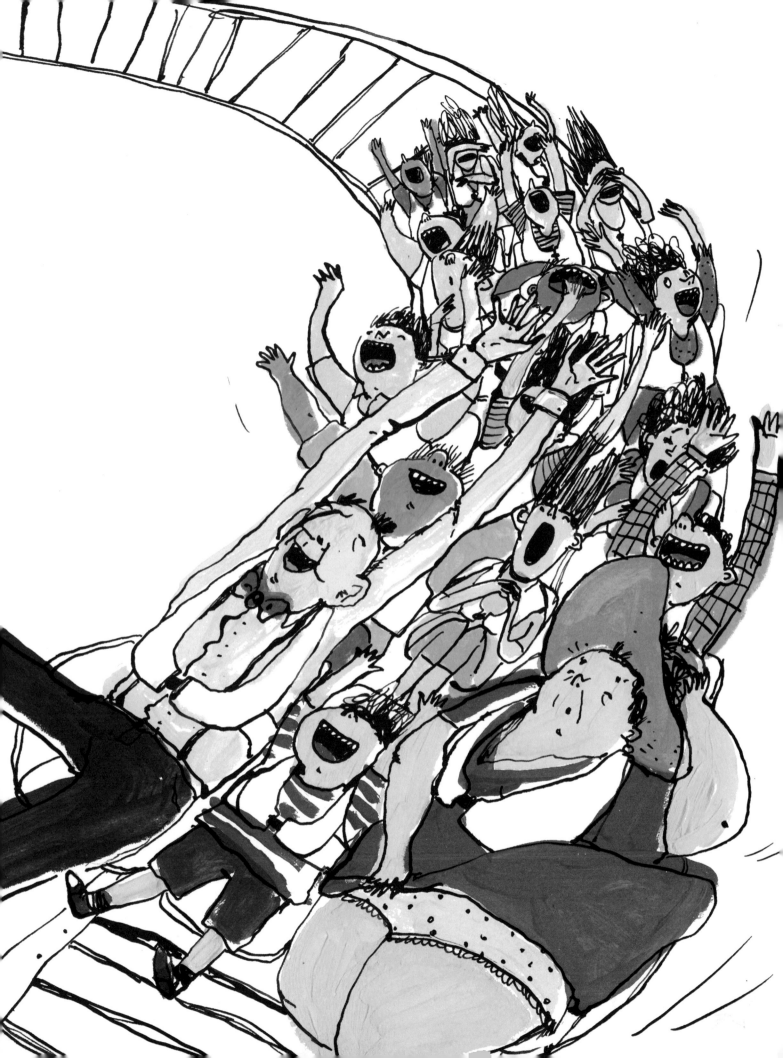

They say that old people are

SLOW,

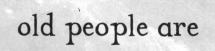

old people are

and old people are

Someone told me old people are

SCARED

of new things,

OLD

PEOPLE

DON'T

. DANCE,

and old people
definitely don't care for

ROMANCE.

They say that old people are

QUIET,

and old people are

NOT AT ALL
ADVENTUROUS.

But I know the
truth about old people.

Old people are . . .

A M A

ZING!